DANITRA BROWN, CLASS CLOWN

By Nikki Grimes

Illustrated by E. B. Lewis

HarperCollins*Publishers*

Amistad

Amistad is an imprint of HarperCollins Publishers Inc.
Danitra Brown, Class Clown
Text copyright © 2005 by Nikki Grimes
Illustrations copyright © 2005 by E. B. Lewis
Manufactured in China.
All rights reserved.
For information address HarperCollins Children's Books,
a division of HarperCollins Publishers,
195 Broadway, New York, NY 10007.
www.harperchildrens.com

Library of Congress Cataloging-in-Publication Data
Grimes, Nikki.   Danitra Brown, class clown / Nikki Grimes ;
illustrated by E. B. Lewis.—1st ed.   p. cm.   Summary: In this story told in a series
of rhyming poems, Zuri faces her fears about starting a new school year with the help
of her free-spirited best friend, Danitra.   ISBN 0-688-17290-3—ISBN 0-688-17291-1
(lib. bdg.)   [1. Schools—Fiction. 2. Best friends—Fiction. 3. Friendship—Fiction.
4. African Americans—Fiction. 5. Stories in rhyme.]   I. Lewis, Earl B., ill. II. Title.
PZ8.3.G8875Dan 2005   [Fic]—dc22   2004003851

Typography by Carla Weise
17 SCP 20 19 18 17 16 15 14
❖
First Edition

To Michelle Green,
in celebration of friendship
—N.G.

To my agents,
Jeff Dwyer and Elizabeth O'Grady.
Thank you for your insight.
—E.B.L.

SCHOOL IS IN

School is in and I remember
How much I detest September:
    New classroom I have to scout
    New teacher to figure out
    New and harder math to learn
    (Numbers that make my stomach churn)
    New bullies to face or fear
    (Perhaps I should slip out of here)
But then, Danitra hops in, grinning
and all my gloomy thoughts go spinning.

"Z" IS FOR ZURI

The first day of school
is always the same.
The new teacher pauses
when she calls my name.
She asks what it means.
It's the moment I dread.
I squirm like a turtle
and tuck in my head.
I whisper the answer
and cringe when I hear
giggles rising and popping
like balloons in my ear.
Then Danitra Brown pokes me
three times in my side.
I lift up my head, and
repeat with more pride,
"My name means beautiful,
wonderful, good.
Anyone with half a brain
would steal it, if she could."

MISS VOLCHEK

Everyone loved Miss Wexler,
the teacher we had last year.
She called us Miss and Mister.
Too bad she's no longer here.

Miss Volchek's our new teacher.
She calls us by our first names.
She treats us like small children,
and nothing is quite the same.

Miss Wexler spoke in whispers.
Miss Volchek raises her voice.
She picks what books we read now.
Miss Wexler gave us a choice.

Miss Volchek gives us quizzes
with no warning in advance,
and still Danitra tells us
that we should give her a chance.

A WORLD AWAY

Miss Volchek warned us not to speak.
"Stop chattering, you two."
But keeping quiet all day was
impossible to do.
Obeying will be easier
beginning with today.
Miss Volchek made Danitra sit
three stinking rows away.

LUNCHTIME

Danitra won't swap
but is willing to share
her lunch box treats.
She doesn't care
that some kids laugh
at her corn bread square
spread with tuna,
or that people stare
at her peanut-butter sandwich
stuffed with pear.
(Her dessert of black olives
is what raises my hair!)
But that's my Danitra,
feasting on fare
nobody else
would even dare.

CLASS CLOWN

Last week, I scribbled one dumb note:
"I think Wardell is cute," I wrote.

I passed it to Danitra Brown,
but Luther snatched it, turned around

and, in a singsong voice, he read
my note. (I wished that I were dead!)

Danitra sprang up from her seat.
She twirled, and leaped, and stomped her feet.

The class laughed at Danitra's dance,
and while they laughed, I had a chance

to grab my note—which was her plan,
though I was slow to understand.

Danitra acted like a clown
for *me*. That's my Danitra Brown.

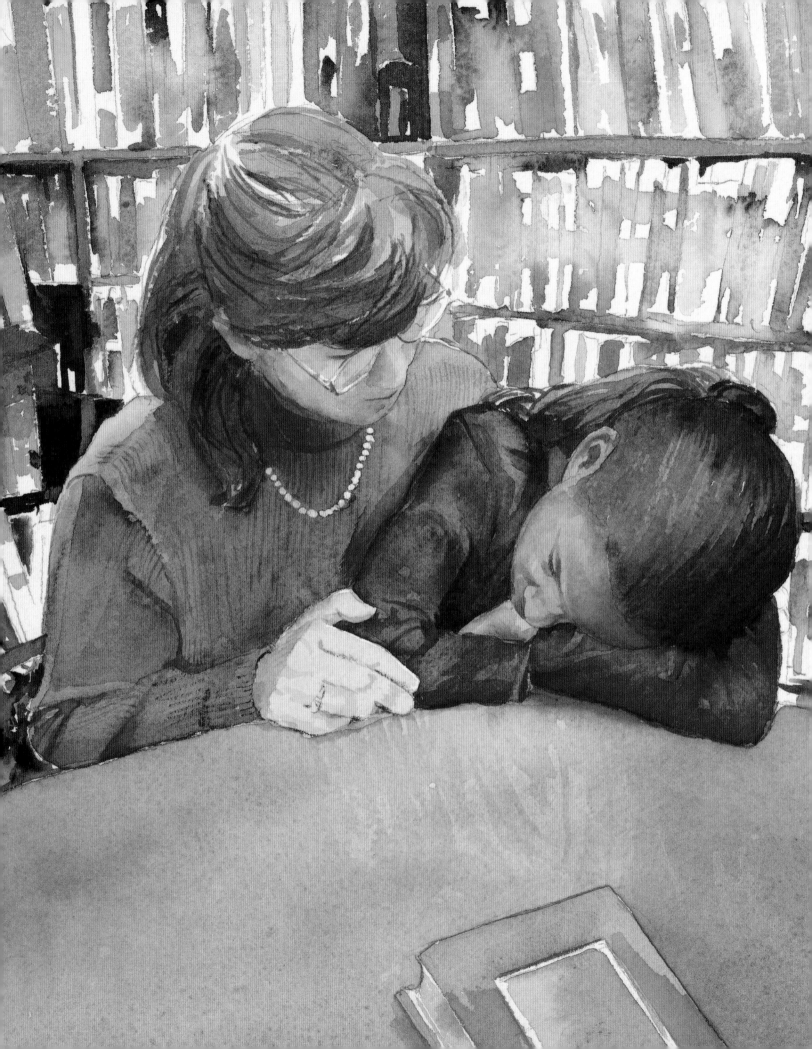

A FRIEND IN NEED

My mom was very sick last month,
I think the whole school knew.
The doctor thought that she might die
and I believed it, too.

For days, I acted unafraid.
I wouldn't even frown.
But then one day, out of the blue
I suddenly broke down.

I cried inside the library.
I hid behind a book.
I felt as if my heart would split.
From head to toe, I shook.

Danitra wasn't there that day.
I felt so all alone
until Miss Volchek pulled me close
as if I were her own.

HOMEWORK

Serious homework requires a snack.
I serve buttered popcorn before we crack
our math books open, then let out a moan.
Danitra says it's too early to groan.
But math problems make my brain cells go numb.
In no time, I'm screaming, "That's it! I'm too dumb!"
"No, you're not!" says Danitra. "So don't fill your head

with ideas like that. Get a tutor instead."
I feel mortified. She reads my mind
and whispers, "We *all* need help sometime."
I sniffle and say, "Tomorrow I'll see
if Miss Volchek has extra time for me."
Meantime, I study my math book again
and finish my homework as best I can.

HOCUS-POCUS

Danitra comes
and calls me from
the window.
I say good-bye
to an afternoon of play
and let her work
her weird magic.

Abracadabra

She says the right words,
waves her pencil,
and math solutions
burst like fireworks
lighting up my mind.

Hocus-pocus

I'm telling you,
it's true.
When Danitra is here,
my math problems disappear
    right
        before
           my eyes.

CLIMB EV'RY MOUNTAIN

I have a solo today.
The glee club
is behind me,
lips puckered
round as quarters,
*ooh-ooh*ing on cue.
I stand front and center
in an all-school assembly,
and my mouth opens,
and I'm not sure
what will come out.
A whimper? A shout?
The right chord
would be nice.
I close my eyes,
soak in the melody,
and drown any doubt.
I sing "Climb Ev'ry Mountain"
and I do.

STOMACHACHE

I have a fever.
I feel a chill.
My stomach aches.
I need a pill.
Danitra says
it's in my mind.
"You'll wake tomorrow
and you'll be fine."
I hope she's wrong.
I need my rest.
I'm way too sick
to take a test.

MATH SCORE

The math exam's been graded
and, though I did my best,
my hands are cold and sweaty.
What if I failed the test?
What if all that tutoring
didn't do the trick?
What if all my studying
didn't help a lick?

What if I get left behind?
What will I do then?
What if I retake this class
and fail all over again?
The teacher calls out, "Jackson."
I rise on wobbly knees
and sleepwalk to Miss Volchek's desk
as slowly as you please.
I take the paper from her hand.
I gulp, then check my score.
I hardly can believe my eyes—
I got an 84!

DANITRA BROWN

One of a kind hairdo
One of a kind smile
Singular appetite
Singular style
Original thinker
Ignoring every trend
Matchless tutor
Matchless friend

HALF AND HALF

The school year is half over
and half of me is glad.
That half can hardly wait till June.
The other half is sad.
My classes will be changing.
I'll move one grade ahead.
I'll sort of miss Miss Volchek.
(You tell her, and you're dead.)
I can't imagine next year will be
half as good as now,
but Danitra and I will find a way
to make it great, somehow.